Barbie as The Princess and the Pauper

MOVIE THEATER AND MUSIC PLAYER STORYBOOK

Adapted by Wendy A. Wax

Reader's Digest Children's Books®

Pleasantville, New York • Montréal, Québec • Bath, United Kingdom

The Princess and the Pauper

Play Song 1

*I*n a mountain village, two baby girls were born the same day. They looked exactly alike except for their hair. One was a blonde princess named Anneliese. The dark-haired girl was named Erika and was born to a poor family.

Disk 1
①

Princess Anneliese grew up in the royal palace with her mother, the Queen, and her pet cat, Serafina.

She spent her days learning her royal
duties with her tutor, Julian. Meanwhile,
Erika worked as a seamstress for mean
 Madame Carp. Her pet cat, Wolfie, kept
Erika company.

One day the Royal Miners told the Queen
that the gold in the mine had run out.
The Queen's trusted advisor,
Preminger, had stolen
the gold. He wanted
to marry Anneliese
so that he could
become king.
The stolen gold
would make
his plan work.

Play
Song
2

The Queen knew none of this, and she had to find a way to take care of her people. So she arranged for Anneliese to marry a rich young king, named Dominick.

Anneliese was miserable about the wedding. And Julian was also unhappy, because he was in love with the Princess.

Preminger was furious! He planned to kidnap Anneliese and then "find" her. *If the girl is missing and I find her, the Queen will be so grateful that she'll let me marry the girl,* he thought. *Then I'll be king!*

To cheer Anneliese up, Julian took her into town one day. There, Anneliese heard a girl singing.

Anneliese dropped a gold coin into the girl's cup, and the two girls looked at each other. It was like looking into a mirror! They were amazed to discover how much alike they looked in nearly every way, except for their hair color and a birthmark on the Princess's shoulder.

That night, Anneliese was kidnapped by the henchmen aiding Preminger with his devious plan! They locked Anneliese and Serafina in an abandoned chalet deep in the forest.

At that moment, Preminger galloped up. "Keep the Princess here until the wedding

to King Dominick is canceled," he ordered his henchmen. "Then we'll see who she marries!"

The next morning, the Queen found a letter from Anneliese. "It says she's run away so she won't have to marry King Dominick!" the Queen gasped. Preminger read the note and smiled to himself. Then he handed the note to Julian.

④

Play Song 4

Julian was suspicious, so he went to the village and asked Erika to pretend to be the Princess. "If Preminger thinks you're Anneliese, I can trick him into revealing where he's hiding the Princess," Julian explained to Erika.

Julian sneaked Erika and Wolfie into the palace, and gave Erika a blonde wig so she would look exactly like Anneliese. He then tutored her in the many things a true (5) princess had to know.

Later that day, Julian entered the throne room with Erika, disguised as the Princess. She apologized for running away. Preminger was shocked. The Queen was delighted. The wedding was back on!

Play Song 5

That night, the real Anneliese and Serafina escaped from the chalet and headed back to the palace. Meanwhile, Preminger walked through the forest, trying to make sense of the day.

"Why didn't the Princess tell the Queen she'd been captured?" he mused. "I must solve this if I am to be king!"

Then he heard a twig crack behind him. Julian was hiding nearby, and he had heard everything! The henchmen 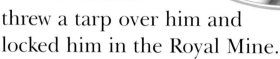 threw a tarp over him and locked him in the Royal Mine.

Anneliese finally reached the palace gate, but the guard would not let her in. "I just saw the Princess eating dinner with the Queen," he said. "Now move along!" So she and Serafina went down to the village and ran into Madame Carp.

Madame Carp dragged Anneliese to the seamstress shop, refusing to believe that this girl was the Princess.

"Get back to work!" she ordered Anneliese, locking her in the store.

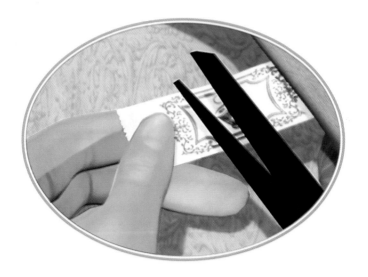

Anneliese sighed—locked up again!

Thinking quickly, she tied her royal ring to Serafina's collar using a label snipped from a dress.

"Take this to the palace, Serafina!" she urged. "When somebody reads the label, it'll lead them here."

The next morning at the dress shop, Anneliese struggled with sewing a dress. Meanwhile, Preminger escorted Erika to meet King Dominick.

"Dominick, will you play the piano for us?" asked the Queen.

"I will," answered Dominick, "if the princess will sing with me."

Erika happily agreed to sing. The two then danced together, quickly falling in love. But the King was falling in love with Erika, not Anneliese!

That evening, a tired Serafina finally reached the palace, but Preminger cornered her and saw the label on the cat's collar. He headed to the dress shop.

Anneliese was relieved to see Preminger. It wasn't until he hustled her into the carriage that she realized he was the one who arranged her earlier kidnapping!

"You were clever to find a double to fool the Queen," Preminger told her. "But not quite clever enough."

Preminger forced the Princess into the mine with Julian. Then he bolted the door and ordered his henchmen to destroy the mine.

As Anneliese looked at Julian, she knew that she had to confess her love to him. Julian felt the same way about Anneliese!

8

Play Song 6

Back at the palace, Preminger rushed into the throne room. "Seize the impostor!" he said, pointing at Erika. "She and Julian hid the real princess in the Royal Mine. I tried to rescue the princess but it was too late. The mine collapsed." He sadly gave Anneliese's ring to the Queen.

Disk 2 (9)

"Only this was found in the rubble."

The Queen checked Erika's shoulder. There was no birthmark on it.

"Throw her in the dungeon!" Preminger ordered. Then he turned to the Queen. He told her how wealthy he was and asked her to marry him. The Queen agreed. She saw no other way to save the kingdom.

Meanwhile, Anneliese and Julian hacked at the rocks blocking the entrance to the mine, but it was hopeless. As Anneliese struggled to move a rock, it broke apart, revealing sparkling purple crystals.

"Julian," she said. "This treasure can save the kingdom! And we can marry!"

Suddenly, an unused mine shaft crashed down into the room. Julian and Anneliese could see daylight! The mine filled up with water, and as the water rose, Julian and Anneliese floated up the mine shaft. They ⑪ headed to the castle, but the wedding had already begun!

In the meantime, Erika had snagged the ⑫ keys and escaped from the dungeon—only to be caught by a guard in the hall. When ⑬ he lifted up his helmet, she saw it was really King Dominick! Erika, King Dominick, Anneliese, and Julian arrived at the castle at the same time.

"Wait!" cried Anneliese. "Stop the wedding, Mother!" She pointed at Preminger. "He stole the gold from the mine."

"The impostor escaped!" said Preminger. But Anneliese showed her birthmark. The Queen hugged her daughter with relief. She realized at last how Preminger had tricked her, and sent him to the dungeon.

"I don't want to waste any more time," said King Dominick to Erika. "Will you be my wife?"

Erika happily agreed.

Anneliese spoke to her mother, "I don't want to marry King Dominick. It's Julian I want to marry."

"But how will we take care of our people?" the Queen asked.

"I found some crystals in the mine, Mother. They are worth enough to take care of our people for a long time," Anneliese answered.

So Erika married Dominick and Anneliese married Julian in a beautiful double wedding. And the two princesses remained friends forever.

16